ISABEL'S SCHOOL ADVENTURE

Adapted by **Sara Miller** • Based on the episode **"Crystal in the Rough"**
written by **Mercedes Valle** for the series created by **Craig Gerber**
Illustrated by **Premise Entertainment**

ABDOBOOKS.COM

Reinforced library bound edition published in 2020 by Spotlight, a division of ABDO, PO Box 398166, Minneapolis, Minnesota 55439. Spotlight produces high-quality reinforced library bound editions for schools and libraries. Published by agreement with Disney Press, an imprint of Disney Book Group.

Printed in the United States of America, North Mankato, Minnesota.
092019   012020

DISNEP PRESS
New York • Los Angeles

THIS BOOK CONTAINS RECYCLED MATERIALS

Library of Congress Control Number: 2019942981

Publisher's Cataloging-in-Publication Data

Names: Miller, Sara; Valle, Mercedes, authors. | Premise Entertainment, illustrator.
Title: Elena of Avalor: Isabel's school adventure / by Sara Miller, and Mercedes Valle; illustrated by
    Premise Entertainment.
Other title: Isabel's school adventure
Description: Minneapolis, Minnesota : Spotlight, 2020. | Series: World of reading level 1
Summary: Isabel tries changing herself in order to fit in after learning her smart ways make her unpopular.
Identifiers: ISBN 9781532143991 (lib. bdg.)
Subjects: LCSH: Elena of Avalor (Television program)--Juvenile fiction. | Schools--Juvenile fiction. |
    Princesses--Juvenile fiction. | Identity--Juvenile fiction. | Readers (Elementary)--Juvenile fiction. | Sisters--
    Juvenile fiction.
Classification: DDC [E]--dc23

Spotlight
A Division of ABDO
abdobooks.com

Isabel is excited for the first day of school! She puts her supplies in her Go-Pack.

Isabel worries about making friends. "Everyone will want to be your friend!" says Elena.

In the classroom, Señorita Marisol introduces Isabel.

Isabel sits next to Quique and Amara. They will study chemistry first. "I love chemistry!" Isabel says. Quique and Amara laugh. They do not like chemistry.

It is time for an experiment.
Isabel measures her ingredients.
Quique does not.

Isabel's experiment works!
Quique's experiment does not.

"Tomorrow is the field trip to Crystal Caverns," Señorita Marisol says. Isabel loves crystals and rocks!

After class, the students play a game.
Quique throws the ball in the hole.
Amara throws and misses.

Isabel has an idea.

She tells Amara to change the angle of her throw. It works! But Quique makes fun of Isabel for being smart.

When Isabel gets home, she feels sad.

"What's wrong?" asks Elena. "I bet you were the smartest in the class."
"I just want kids to like me," Isabel says. Then she has an idea.

The next morning, Isabel
seems very different.

In class, Isabel does not measure her
ingredients.
"Watch this," she says.
"Cool," says Quique.

Elena brings Isabel's Go-Pack to school. Señorita Marisol invites Elena on the field trip.

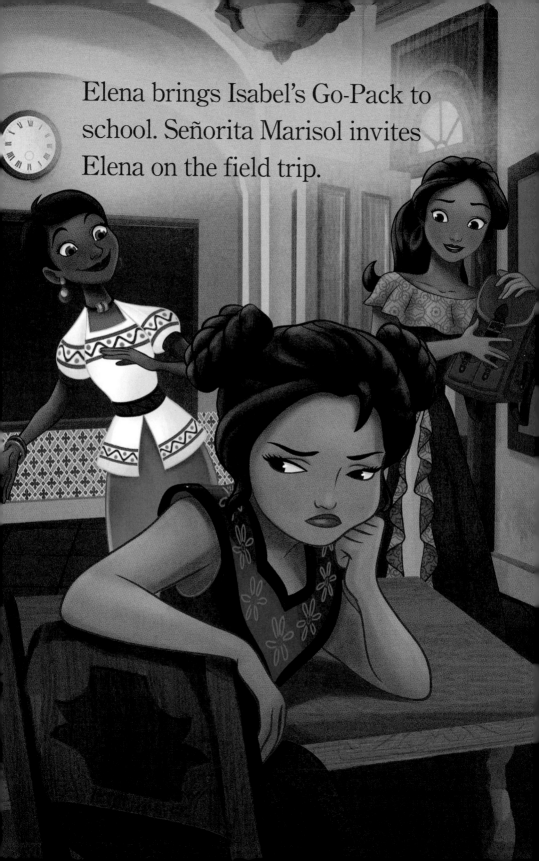

At Crystal Caverns, Quique makes jokes. Amara and Isabel laugh.

Elena asks Isabel why she is being rude.
Isabel shrugs. "I changed myself.
Now I have friends."
"True friends like you for who you are,"
says Elena.

Quique spots a closed-off area.
"Let's go!" he says.

As the friends explore, they hear a CRACK! The crystal floor breaks! They fall through!

They land in a river on a giant lily pad. "HELP!" they shout.

Elena hears them shouting. She rushes to find them. She uses Isabel's jump rope to climb down.

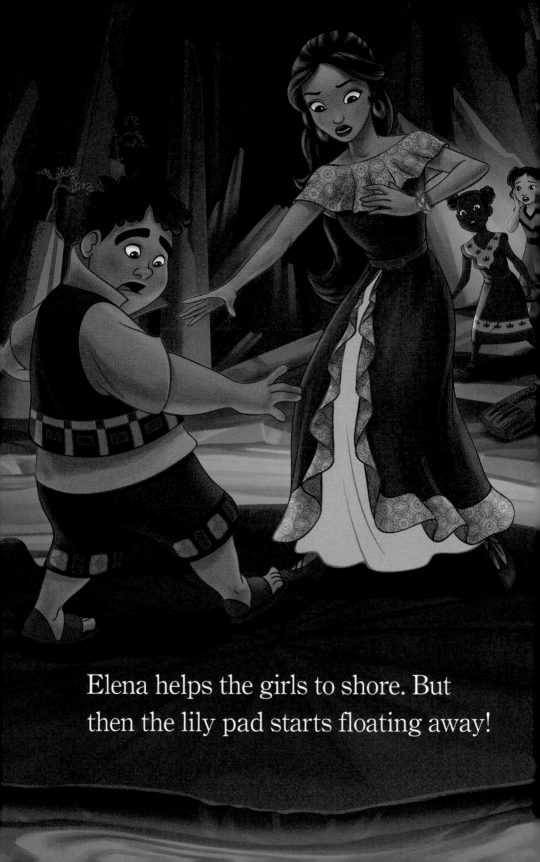

Elena helps the girls to shore. But
then the lily pad starts floating away!

Isabel has an idea. The girls run
under a huge crystal. Isabel tells
Amara to knock it down.

Amara shoots and misses. Isabel tells her to change the angle of her shot.

It works! The crystal falls into the river. Elena and Quique use it to cross to shore.

"Isa!" cries Elena.
"Sorry for the trouble I made," says Isabel.
Elena smiles. "See? You saved us by being yourself!"

"Now how do we get out of here?"
asks Quique.
Isabel smiles at her friends.
"I have an idea!"